AMANDA HALL studied illustration at Cambridge School of Art
and started her career as a children's illustrator in the late 1970s.
Her books include *The Barefoot Book of Animal Tales*, written by Naomi Adler,
Stories from the Sea by James Riordan and *Sunday, Moonday* by Cherry Gilchrist
(all published by Barefoot) and Jamila Gavin's *Our Favourite Stories*,
Barbara Baumgartner's *All My Shining Silver* and *Good as Gold*
(all Dorling Kindersley). *Robi Dobi*, by Madhur Jaffrey (Pavilion)
won the U.S. Parents' Choice Silver Award in 1997.
Among Amanda's more recent publications are *The Storytelling Star*
by James Riordan (Pavilion) and *The Hard to Swallow Tale*
of Jonah and the Whale by Joyce Denham (Lion).
The Stolen Sun is her first book for Frances Lincoln

For Lisa, plentifully.
Also for Ben and Melissa – A.H.

First published in Great Britain in 2002 by
Frances Lincoln Limited, 4 Torriano Mews
Torriano Avenue, London NW5 2RZ

First paperback edition 2003

British Library Cataloguing in Publication Data available on request

ISBN 0-7112-1808-0 hardback
ISBN 0-7112-1844-7 paperback

Set in Plantin Italic

Printed in Singapore
1 3 5 7 9 8 6 4 2

The Stolen Sun

A Story of Native Alaska

Amanda Hall

FRANCES LINCOLN

A Note on the Story

The following themes woven into this story can be found in *The Eskimo about Bering Strait* by Edward William Nelson (Smithsonian Institute, 1983), based on the 18th Annual Report of the Bureau of American Ethnology (Government Printing Office, 1899), These themes form an important part of Native Alaskan belief and culture.

Raven creates the world, teaching the people how to live.

Music accompanies the creation.

Raven stresses the importance of respect for life, which the people ignore.

As a punishment, Raven steals the sun and flies to the 'sky land'.

A feather falls from Raven and is carried from ancient myth to recent past when a woman swallows it.

The woman has a baby who, being part-raven, is destined to regain the sun from his angry father.

The boy's journey begins with the raven mask.

The song leads the boy on and teaches him about the ancient knowledge.

Once upon a time, before ice and before snow, the sky arched like a giant tent over the top of the world. Higher still, in a land above the sky, lived Raven.

In those days there was a hole in the sky linking our world with Raven's. One day Raven flew down through the hole to see what lay below.

To his astonishment he found a world of mountains, rivers and forests, on which the sun shone brightly. But there were no creatures in it. So Raven created animals and people, birds and fishes, and he gave a song to the people, to remind them to love and respect the life around them.

As time passed, the people living on the Earth grew greedy. They no longer respected the life they had been asked to care for. They muttered and argued, they captured and killed, until Raven's song was no more than a whisper.

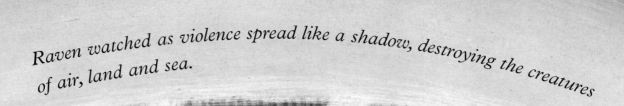

Raven watched as violence spread like a shadow, destroying the creatures of air, land and sea.

Raven grew angry. With a great shriek, he tore the shining sun from its place in the sky. Back he flew through the sky-hole with the sun tucked under his wing, and there he hid the sun in a secret place, leaving the land below to freeze in the silver light of the moon.

Raven vowed never to return to Earth and, plucking one small farewell feather from his breast, he left it to float on the wind as he flew away.

Who knows how long the tiny feather drifted in the cold, dark air?

Down, down, down it floated, and landed on an icy stream.

One cold morning, a woman went to fetch water. She lifted the ladle to her lips and did not see the small black feather floating in the water as she drank.

That night she dreamed of dark fluttering wings, and the raven's forgotten song echoed through her dream.

In time the woman gave birth to a baby boy. He was as silent and beautiful as night itself, and she named him Little Darkness.

As she rocked him in her arms, she sang him her dream, and the tiny baby listened intently, gazing up at her with his dark, dark eyes.

Little Darkness grew to be a fine, brave boy, but although he laughed and played

like other children, his mother felt that he was somehow different.

One day Little Darkness went to the ice to fish, and saw a dark shape nearby. It was a curious mask shaped like a bird's head. Little Darkness touched it. As he did so, a long-forgotten song breathed across the ice, making the surface shimmer and shimmer. Little Darkness lifted the mask over his head.

As he pulled the mask over his face, a great sound filled the sky. Little Darkness felt himself full of power. His shoulders began to ache. Something was growing on his back. He had wings!

Then he was flying up and up, following the song that called him.

Higher and higher went the song and the winged boy, until they came to the hole in the sky. The song floated through, but when Little Darkness tried to follow, there was a terrible screeching from up above. It was a giant raven whirling down, trying to catch hold of the intruder.

Little Darkness held up his hands to shield his face. Gasping, he pulled off the mask and saw a cloud of dark feathers swirling in front of him. He fell back, and as he did so, his wings disappeared. Then all was blackness.

Slowly Little Darkness awoke. At first he thought he was in his mother's arms, for he felt her warmth and heard her lullaby. But no – he was floating through the air. Cradled by a gentle mist, he was carried up through the sky-hole.

Above the sky he drifted, across strange valleys and seas,
until the mist set him down at the foot of a steep mountain.
It was made entirely of ice, and at its centre a dim light glowed.

Little Darkness had never seen light before. It looked warm and bright, and he wanted it. Taking his axe from his belt, he began to hack his way up the frozen mountainside towards the light.

While he hacked, Little Darkness sang – at first in a small voice, but as he climbed, his voice grew. The warmth of his song made the wall wet against his hands. Above him he could hear the screech of the raven, but still he did not stop.

Water began to stream down around him, threatening to wash away his foothold. Ice crashed down the mountainside, but he sang out even louder.

And as he sang, the glow from the mountain grew stronger. Now the icy walls were no more than a thin glassy veil. One more blow and the sun would be released. But just as Little Darkness raised his axe to strike, the last piece of ice broke away.

From up above, Raven saw his son falling.
No! He must not die! Down Raven swooped,
lifting Little Darkness to safety.
"Up on my back," he commanded, and
Little Darkness sat holding on to the short
feathers around Raven's neck, unafraid now
of the fierce beak or the sharp claws.

Raven flew to the sun and grasped it firmly.
Off they flew, back over the seas and valleys,
back to the hole in the sky. Raven dived down
through it and cast the huge fiery sphere up
into the sky again, where it blazed brightly,
lighting up the whole world.

Down on the Earth below, a mother gazed
up at the brilliant glittering sky.
"Little Darkness!" she cried.
"You are safe! And I can
hear our song again!"

OTHER PICTURE BOOKS IN PAPERBACK
FROM FRANCES LINCOLN

MARIANA AND THE MERCHILD
Caroline Pitcher
Illustrated by Jackie Morris
Old Mariana longs for friendship, but she is feared by the village children
and fearful of the sea-wolves hiding in the sea-caves near her hut.
Then one day her lonely life changes when she finds a Merbaby inside a crabshell …
A magically-illustrated folk tale from Chile.

Suitable for National Curriculum English – Reading, Key Stages 1 and 2
Scottish Guidelines English Language – Reading, Levels B and C

ISBN 0-7112-1464-6 £5.99

THE COMING OF NIGHT
James Riordan
Illustrated by Jenny Stow
When the great river goddess Yemoya sends her daughter Aje to marry a chief
in the Land of Shining Day, Aje pines for the dark shadows of her mother's realm.
So her husband sends Crocodile and Hippopotamus down to the river
to bring back a sackful of Night …
A Yoruba creation myth from West Africa that will delight young readers.

Suitable for National Curriculum English – Reading, Key Stages 1 and 2
Scottish Guidelines English Language – Reading, Levels B and C

ISBN 0-7112-1378-X £5.99

RAINBOW BIRD
Eric Maddern
Illustrated by Adrienne Kennaway
"I'm boss for Fire," growls rough, tough Crocodile Man, and he keeps the rest
of the world cold and dark, until one day clever Bird Woman sees her opportunity
and seizes it. An Aboriginal fire myth, lit with glowing illustrations.

Suitable for National Curriculum English – Reading, Key Stage 1
Scottish Guidelines English Language – Reading, Levels A and B

ISBN 0-7112-0898-0 £5.99

Frances Lincoln titles are available from all good bookshops.
Prices are correct at time of publication, but may be subject to change.